Zombie Cat

To my wonderful husband and best friend, James Duffett-Smith —I.A.

To my parents, Denyse and Jeremy —B.S.

Skyhorse books may be purchased in bulk at special discounts for sales promotion, corporate gifts, fund-raising, or educational purposes. Special editions can also be created to specifications. For details, contact the Special Sales Department, Skyhorse Publishing, 307 West 36th Street, 11th Floor, New York, NY 10018 or info@skyhorsepublishing.com.

Skyhorse® is a registered trademark of Skyhorse Publishing, Inc.®, a Delaware corporation.

Visit our website at www.skyhorsepublishing.com.

10 9 8 7 6 5 4 3 2 1

Printed in China

Library of Congress Cataloging-in-Publication Data

Atherton, Isabel.
  Zombie cat : the tale of a decomposing kitty / written by Isabel Atherton ; illlustrated by Bethany Straker.
    p. cm.
  ISBN 978-1-61608-884-2 (hardcover : alk. paper)
  1. Cats--Humor. 2. Cats--Pictorial works. I. Title.
  PN6231.C23A84 2012
  818'.5402--dc23
                    2012012962

Cover design by Brian Peterson
Cover illustrations by Bethany Straker

Paperback ISBN: 978-1-5107-7370-7
Ebook ISBN: 978-1-62087-488-2

Zombie Cat

The Tale of a Decomposing Kitty

Written by Isabel Atherton

Illustrated by Bethany Straker

Skyhorse Publishing

Zombie Cat wasn't always one of the undead. He'd once been called Tiddles and had normal cat pursuits—chasing mice, lounging around, and chatting up female kitties.

Sadly, this was all about to change. A nuclear power plant spill had not only had a detrimental effect on the local wildlife, but was about to change Tiddles's cat life forever.

It was while Tiddles was casing out a rather sorrowful-looking field mouse that he realized something was horribly wrong. The mouse bit him.

Four hours later and with a catnip hangover from hell, Tiddles was Tiddles no more. Zombie Cat was born. (Make that *reborn* or *reanimated*. Whatever you call something that was once dead and is now inexplicably shuffling around mewing strangely.)

Gone was his lustrous coat and gleaming white teeth. Instead, the new Tiddles was ratty, mangy, and well, quite honestly, falling apart. He was on his last legs, except his last legs had expired hours ago.

His mind also seemed very hazy. As he shuffled along on his paws, one thought and one thought alone was in his mind: braaiiiinnnsssss!! Yes, the gloopy gray stuff in your head was on Zombie Cat's zombie mind.

Now, as one of the undead, you'd think that Zombie Cat would be stumbling after every living thing. Well, this wasn't the case—Zombie Cat still had a conscience. As he passed a group of his fellow undead felines devouring a little girl on a tricycle, he shuffled home with his rotting nose turned up (this was partly due, however, to the fact that it was starting to come away from his face).

Jake, his owner, was shocked to find that his beloved Tiddles was reanimated roadkill. At first he boarded up the cat flap and bolted all the windows and doors in an attempt to rid himself of this horrible monster-cat vision.

The Zombie Cat mewing at Jake's door kept him awake for days. He peeked out his window and saw his former pet in pieces, and his heart melted. Yes, Tiddles was now a zombie, but he'd been a good companion. Jake needed to do something.

Tentatively opening the front door, Jake picked up the wriggling pieces of Zombie Cat. He proceeded to sew his Tiddles back together. It was a hack job, he admitted to himself, but it would just have to do. Who knew how long a zombie cat could unlive for?

Jake and his monstrous cat reached an understanding. Zombie Cat could stay
and live with his owner just as long as he promised not to eat him. They
would spend their days in quiet, companionable silence while the zombie apocalypse
played out around them and the rest of the neighbors were eaten.

These days Jake is the sole survivor on his street. The other zombies seem to sense the presence (or smell) of something undead and keep away. Although suffering the odd paw falling off, Zombie Cat can be found on his kitty laptop, chatting to his fellow feline undead. They only ever seem to write one thing: "Braiiiinnnnnsss!!"

It is now day 38 of the zombie apocalypse. Most of the undead are dying out (again), and Jake and Zombie Cat can be seen many an evening doing impressions of Michael Jackson's "Thriller" video.

But not all is what it seems. ZC, as he now wants to be called, has been looking at Jake as a rather tasty morsel of late . . .

Isabel Atherton would like to thank the following people:

Heartfelt thanks to my amazing husband, James Duffett-Smith, for believing in my quirky ideas and for laughing along with me. Day 38 of the zombie apocalypse was your wonderful, inspired suggestion. To my parents, David and Pamela Atherton, for encouraging me to be creative all my life. My brilliant brother—Philip Atherton. It was your cat, Wellington, that has led to my love of cats. I could not have realized this book without my friend and the awesome illustrator of *Zombie Cat*—Bethany Straker. To my wonderful friend and editor, Julie Matysik, for seeing the charm of publishing an adult picture book about a zombie cat. Here's to many more nights quaffing cocktails in NYC together, especially at Halloween time! And to Tony Lyons for commissioning the project and for saying that *Zombie Cat* tickled his funny bone. And to all of the wonderful people at Skyhorse who have helped realize this book. Thanks to Catty and his catnip, Angie Thomas for just being awesome and for making us the *Zombie Cat* book trailers, and to Rosemary O'Brien, our simply amazing publicist. To my wonderful friends in Whitstable—you know who you all are, and thanks for supporting me! And thank you to our readers—I will raise a Zombie cocktail to you all!

Bethany Straker would like to thank the following people:

Isabel, to you I owe the biggest debt of gratitude for this project, this opportunity, and this adventure. For changing the direction of my career by sharing your book with me, I cannot thank you enough! You just seemed to know how much it would suit me. To my new and unimaginably important husband, Jof; thank you for listening, helping, advising, and believing in me. To my wonderful parents and sister, for tolerating my lifelong obsession with illustration throughout success and failure, and for never, never telling me to give up. To everyone at Skyhorse for sharing our vision and giving us this gift, and to Julie for being as enthusiastic as we are about it! And not forgetting you, Marvin the rabbit.